Cambridge
Early Years

Learner's Book 1B

Alison Borthwick, Gill Budgell, Kathryn Harper, Philippa Hines,
Claire Medwell & Cherri Moseley

Contents

Note to parents and practitioners — 3

Block 3: Food and things we grow
Let's Explore — 4
Communication and Language — 8
Mathematics — 19

Block 4: Animals
Let's Explore — 21
Communication and Language — 25
Mathematics — 38

Acknowledgements — 40

Note to parents and practitioners

This Learner's Book provides activities and stories to support the second term of Let's Explore, Communication and Language, and Mathematics for Cambridge Early Years 1.

Activities can be used at school or at home. Children will need support from an adult. Additional guidance about activities can be found in the **For practitioners** boxes.

Some activities use stickers. The stickers can be found in the section in the middle of this book.

Stories are provided for children to enjoy looking at and listening to. Children are not expected to be able to read the stories themselves.

Children will encounter the following characters within this book. You could ask children to point to the characters when they see them on the pages, and say their names.

The Learner's Book activities support the Teaching Resource activities. The Teaching Resource provides step-by-step coverage of the Cambridge Early Years curriculum and guidance on how the Learner's Book activities develop the curriculum learning statements.

Hi, my name is Mia.

Find us on the front covers doing lots of fun activities.

Hi, my name is Gemi.

Hi, my name is Rafi.

Hi, my name is Kiho.

Block 3 Food and things we grow

What's in the garden?
Choose stickers and say.

For practitioners
Children look and put the matching pictures in place, e.g., tomato to table. Explore the picture together, looking for food that grows above the ground, food that grows under the ground and food that children like to eat. Read and encourage children to share their responses to Kiho's question.

Where do they grow?

Follow the lines.

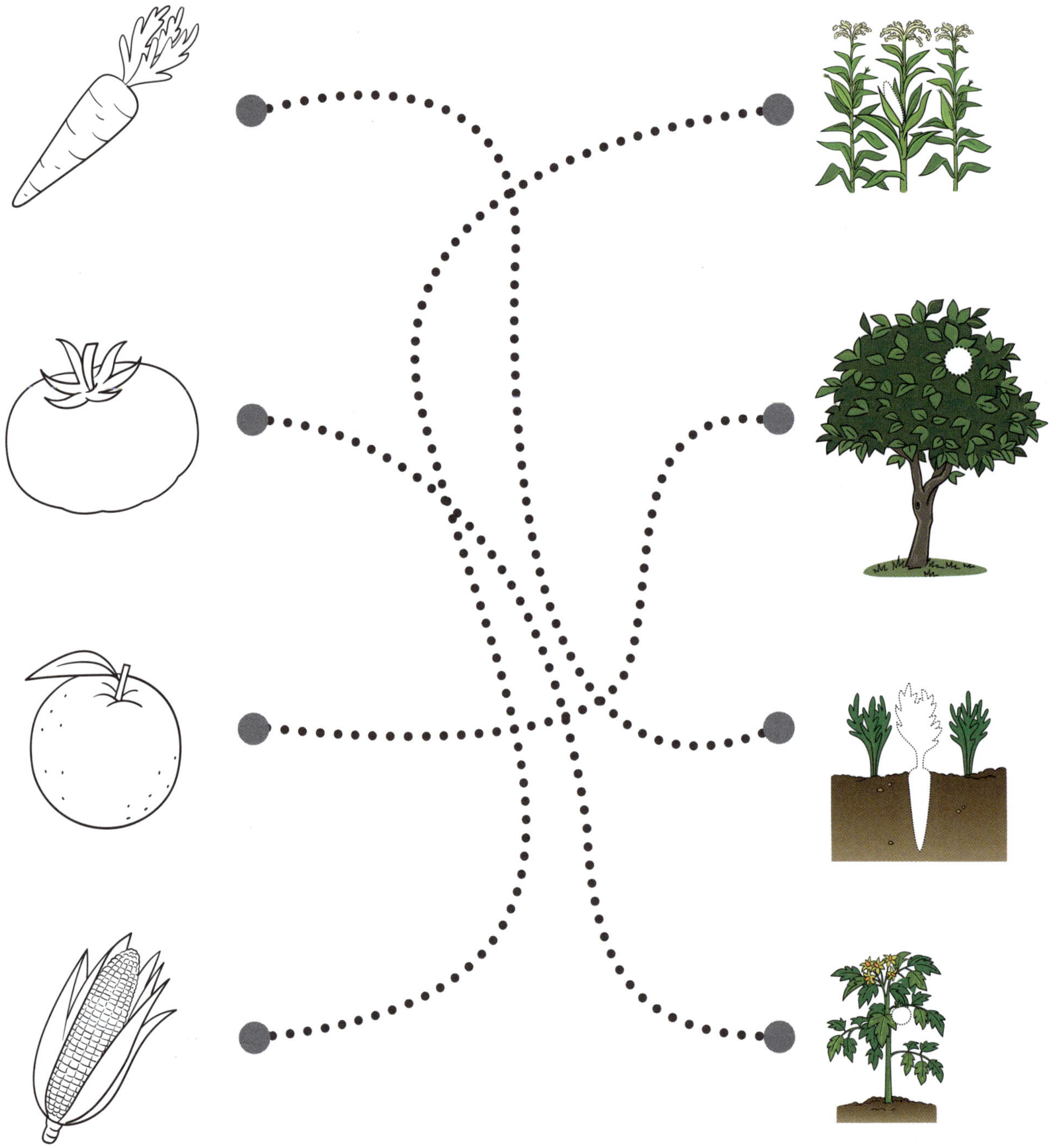

For practitioners

Children trace with their finger or use a pencil to match the fruits and vegetables on the left-hand side to the plants on the right-hand side. They can then colour them in. Ask *Have you seen or eaten any of these fruits and vegetables? What other fruits and vegetables do you know?* Talk about fruit and vegetable plants in your local environment.

What is dangerous in the kitchen?
Stick and say.

For practitioners
Children circle or put stickers on the things that are dangerous in the kitchen. Ask *Why is this dangerous?* Talk about how this kitchen can be made safer. Ask *Which things in the kitchen are electric? How should we be safe around electricity?* Talk about any safety rules you have in your classroom about using electricity.

Fruity Song

Strawberries are red and sweet.
(hold up strawberry/red card)

They're my favourite fruit to eat!

Orange mangoes are so yummy.
(hold up mango/orange card)

"Thank you, thank you!" says my tummy!
(smile and rub tummy)

Bananas and kiwis, oranges too.
(hold up banana, kiwi and orange)

Fruit is yummy and good for you!
(point to a friend)

Find the fruit basket

Follow the lines.

Trace the lines to match each fruit to its basket. Say the fruit names.

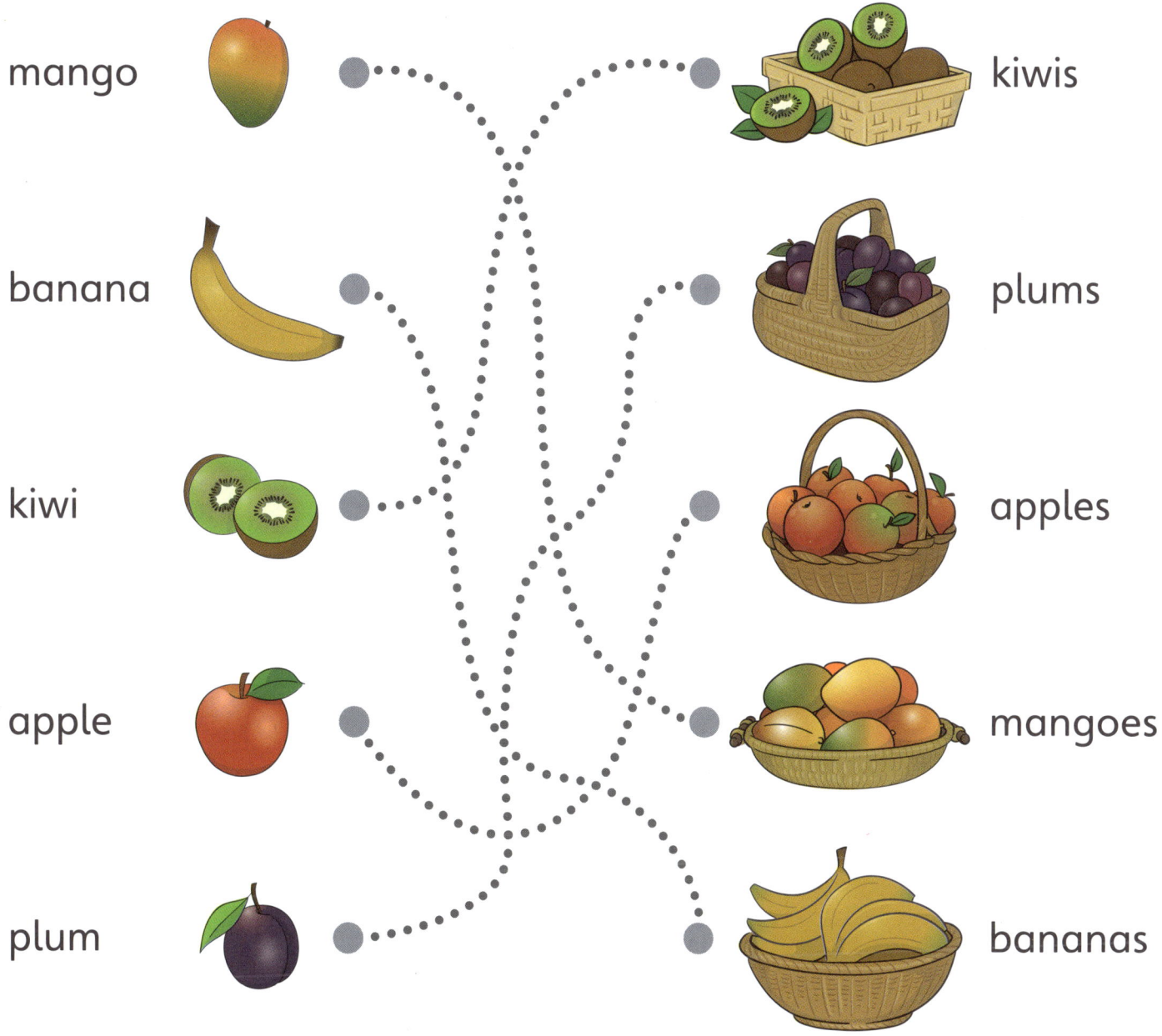

mango

banana

kiwi

apple

plum

kiwis

plums

apples

mangoes

bananas

For practitioners
Encourage children to use visual cues using both pictures and words.
Children should use their finger to carefully follow each line to arrive at the matching fruit basket.

The Last Lemon
by Alison Hawes

"I can't get the last lemon," said the elephant.

"I can help you," said the goat.
"I can get on your back."

"I can't get the last lemon," said the goat.

"I can help you," said the monkey.
"I can get on your back."

"I can't get the last lemon," said the monkey.

"I can help you," said the squirrel. "I can get on your back."

"I can get the last lemon!" said the squirrel.

Picture time

Stick and say.

Stick in pictures of fruits you like to eat.

For practitioners

Children may look in old magazines for pictures of fruits, or take photos. Provide necessary resources such as scissors (for supervised use) and glue, and encourage children to use appropriate vocabulary to describe what they are doing.

The Last Lemon

Point and say.

Retell the story in the correct order.

For practitioners
If necessary, revisit the story again. Encourage children to retell the story in the correct order using the language of the text where possible.

Ouch! Crash!

Spot the difference.

Look at the two pictures. Circle five differences.

For practitioners

Encourage children to recognise or remember the words *ouch* and *crash* from the story. Ask them to find these words on the page, and then look for the differences in the pictures. They may point to or circle the differences in Picture 1.

Feed the animals

Match.

Are there enough watermelons for the elephants to have one each?

Are there enough bamboo sticks for the pandas to have one each?

For practitioners
Children draw a line between each animal and an item of food. Are there enough items for all of the animals to have one each?

Does it have two legs?
Sort.

For practitioners
Children draw lines to show which living things should be in the circle (living things with only two legs).

Block 4 Animals

Look at the animals!
Choose stickers and say.

Stickers for pages 4–5

Stickers for page 7

Stickers for pages 20–21

Stickers for page 39

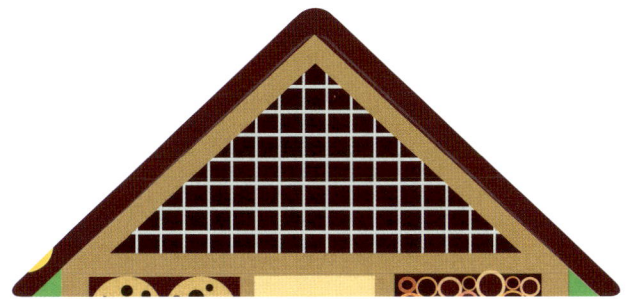

Growing up
Join the dots.

For practitioners
Children trace the lines to complete the picture. Talk about how the duckling will one day look like its daddy as it will grow to be an adult duck over time. Ask children to think about how they are similar and different to their parents. Children can colour in the finished picture.

Bug hunt
Circle and say.

For practitioners
Children find and circle the bugs and worms in the picture. Talk with them about the different characteristics of each bug and where they like to live. Ask *What bugs can you see?* Children find and circle the bugs and worms in the picture. Ask them what they know about the different characteristics of each bug and where they like to live.

Scratch and Sniff Bear by James Carter

The bear came down
   from the mountain
      yawning the morning away

And scratching
   and sniffing
and stretching
   and itching
and fishing
   for most of the day

The bear went
   into the forest
      hoping to find some tea

And stuffing
   and sticking
and picking
   and licking
the honey
   he took from a tree

The bear went back
to the mountain
    yawning from having his fun

And hopping
   and skipping
and humming
   and singing
and happy
   with food in his tum
with honey and fish
   So *YUM!*

Bear questions
Read and say.

Where is each bear?

What is each bear doing?

For practitioners
Point to the words as you read the questions with or for the child.
Encourage children to discuss the pictures, talking about both settings and actions. Revisit the poem as necessary.

The bear

Draw and say.

Draw the bear doing one of the actions from the rhyme.

For practitioners

Help children to decide which action from the rhyme they are going to draw. Then encourage them to talk about their drawing and say what the bear is doing.

Little Tiger Hu Can Roar

by Gabby Pritchard and Galia Bernstein

Little Tiger Hu was very happy. "I can ROAR," he said. It was a BIG and SCARY roar! "I can play a game," he said.

Tiger Hu saw Elephant. Slowly, slowly he went through the long grass. "One, two, three, four … "

"HELP!" shouted Hippo and he jumped into the river.

Little Tiger Hu saw Monkey. Slowly, slowly he climbed up a tree. "One, two, three, four … "

"HELP!" shouted Monkey and he ran up a big tree.

Little Tiger Hu saw Hare.
Slowly, slowly he went over a bridge …
… into a green field.
"One, two, three, four … "

"Hello, Little Tiger Hu," said Hare.

"Why aren't you scared?" said Little Tiger Hu.
"You are silly," said Hare.
"Babies are not scary,
even if they have a big roar."

"We can play a new game,"
said Little Tiger Hu.

Little Tiger Hu and Hare went to play in the forest.

ROAR!

Look and say.

Make a ROAR sound each time you see the word *ROARRR!*

For practitioners
Encourage children to first point to and name each animal. Children point to the word *ROARRR!* in each picture. Model an example with sound before asking children to do the same for each instance.

Little Tiger Hu's tracks

Join the dots.

Retell the story.

For practitioners
Encourage children to join the dots with their finger or using a pencil as they retell the story. Prompt them as necessary, e.g., *Where did Little Tiger Hu go first/next?*, etc.

Spot the shape!
Find and say.

For practitioners
Children talk about which blocks have been used to make the cat. Challenge children to say how the blocks at the bottom of the page are different in the picture. For example, *the legs are the same shape as the body, but a different way round.*

Which shapes can you see?
Choose stickers and say.

For practitioners
Children look and put the missing shapes in place to complete the picture. Ask them to describe the shapes they can see.

Acknowledgements

The authors and publishers acknowledge the following sources of copyright material and are grateful for the permissions granted. While every effort has been made, it has not always been possible to identify the sources of all the material used, or to trace all copyright holders. If any omissions are brought to our notice, we will be happy to include the appropriate acknowledgements on reprinting.

The Last Lemon by Alison Hawes, illustrated by Tamara Anegón, Cambridge Reading Adventures, © Cambridge University Press and UCL Institute of Education, 2016.

'Scratch and Sniff Bear' from *A Ticket to Kalamazoo!* by James Carter, illustrated by Neal Layton, Otter-Barry Books. Used by permission of the publisher.

Little Tiger Hu Can Roar by Gabby Pritchard, illustrated by Galia Bernstein, Cambridge Reading Adventures, © Cambridge University Press and UCL Institute of Education, 2016.

Thanks to the following artists at Beehive Illustration:
Lays Bittencourt, Katharine Henry, Tamara Joubert, Jo Litchfield, Sarah Pitt.

Cover characters by Becky Davies (The Bright Agency)